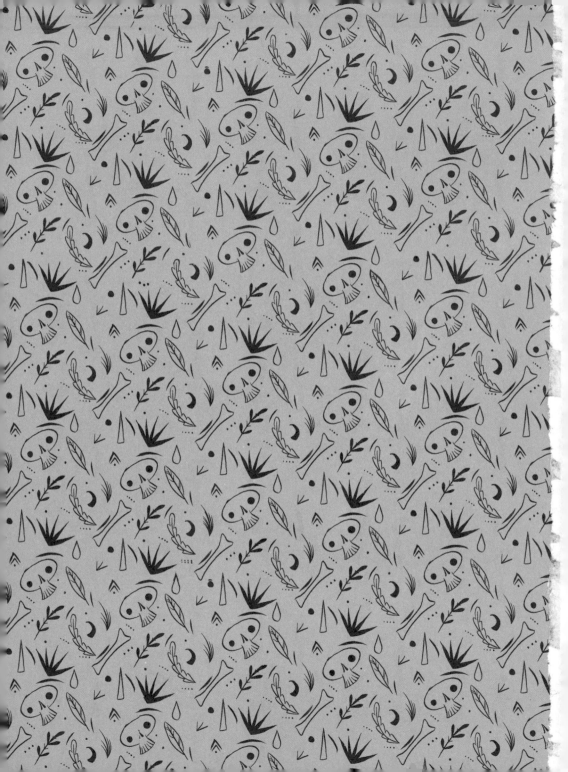

MONSTERS
YOU
SHOULD
KNOW

MONSTERS YOU SHOULD KNOW

EMMA SANCARTIER

CHRONICLE BOOKS

SAN FRANCISCO

Library of Congress Cataloging-in-Publication Data

Names: SanCartier, Emma, author.
Title: Monsters you should know / Emma SanCartier.
Description: San Francisco: Chronicle Books, [2018]
Identifiers: LCCN 2017061275 | ISBN 9781452167770 (hardcover : alk. paper)
Subjects: LCSH: Monsters--Folklore.
Classification: LCC GR825 .S249 2018 | DDC 001.944--dc23 LC
record available at https://lccn.loc.gov/2017061275

Manufactured in China

Design by Lizzie Vaughan

10 9 8 7 6 5 4 3 2

Chronicle books and gifts are available at special quantity discounts to corporations,
professional associations, literacy programs, and other organizations. For details
and discount information, please contact our corporate/premiums department at
corporatesales@chroniclebooks.com or at 1-800-759-0190.

Chronicle Books LLC
680 Second Street
San Francisco, California 94107
www.chroniclebooks.com

INTRODUCTION

The monstrous beasts you're
about to meet exist in folklore
and legends from around the
world. Strange and fantastic, and
sometimes even a little familiar,
many of them have been feared
for centuries. So be sure to take
extra care in your adventures...

BAKU

You may meet this

DREAM-EATER

in Japan...

If you suffer from

NIGHTMARES,

call its name to devour them.

Call too often and it will eat your

HOPES AND DREAMS

as well.

COCKATRICE

This European creature

is born when a

REPTILE

hatches a

ROOSTER EGG.

They have

POISONOUS

breath...

And a gaze that will turn you to

STONE.

SIGBIN

Beware this

VAMPIRIC CREATURE

from the Philippines…

It can

DRAIN YOUR BLOOD

by biting down on your shadow.

You will know its approach by the ominous

CLAPPING

of its

GIANT EARS.

ELOKO

It's unlikely

you'll ever see this

LEAFY CREATURE

deep in the Congo rainforest…

But if you wander into its territory, you may hear the

SOOTHING RING

of its bell.

SHURALE

This

ODD
CREATURE

lives deep in

THE WOODS

of Eastern Europe.

They love to play games and will

TICKLE YOU...

to DEATH.

BONNACON

From the **FRONT,** this Macedonian beast is quite **HARMLESS...**

But never sneak up

BEHIND IT!

Its

ACIDIC DUNG

can be fired at will.

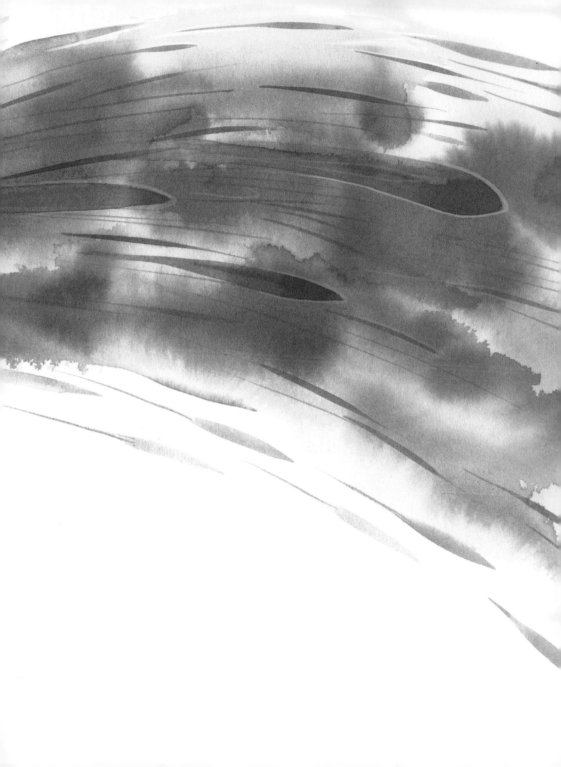

KELPIE

If you spot a

BEAUTIFUL HORSE

swimming in the middle of a

SCOTTISH LAKE...

Don't be

TEMPTED

by its invitation to ride it…

It's less

BEAUTIFUL

than you may think.

PADFOOT

When walking in England at

NIGHT,

if you hear the sound of

CHAINS...

It's already

TOO LATE.

GULON

This Scandinavian

BEAST

is only the size of

A DOG...

But it can kill and eat creatures

TEN TIMES

its size.

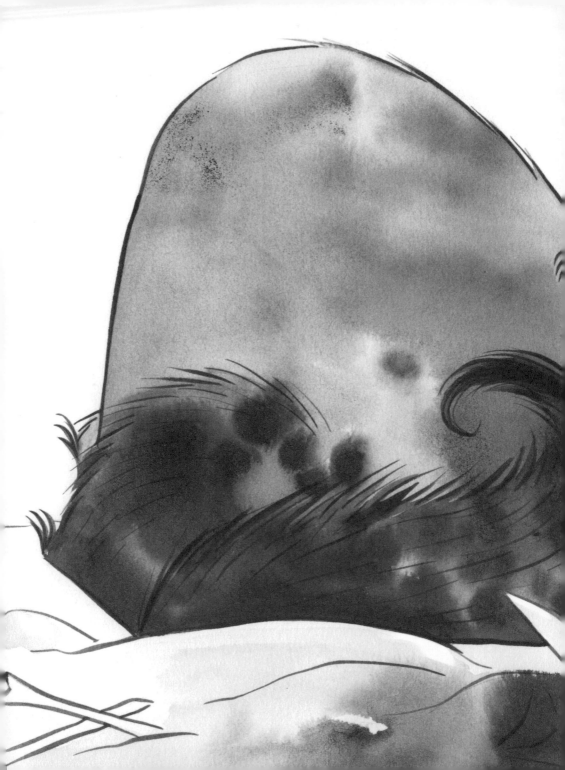

It has

NO SELF-CONTROL.

SQUONK

This American beast

is one of the

UGLIEST

in the world.

It spends most of its time

CRYING AND HIDING

from judgmental gazes.

GUMIHO

This Korean

NINE-TAILED FOX

may catch you

UNAWARES...

It will take the form of a beautiful woman to

SEDUCE YOU...

In order to eat

YOUR LIVER.

IHUAIVULU

This

ENORMOUS DRAGON

lives in

VOLCANOES

in South America.

It can breathe

HUGE WAVES
OF FIRE....

And has

FAR

too many heads.

ADARO

This

SPIRIT

can be found in the

WATERS

of the Pacific Islands.

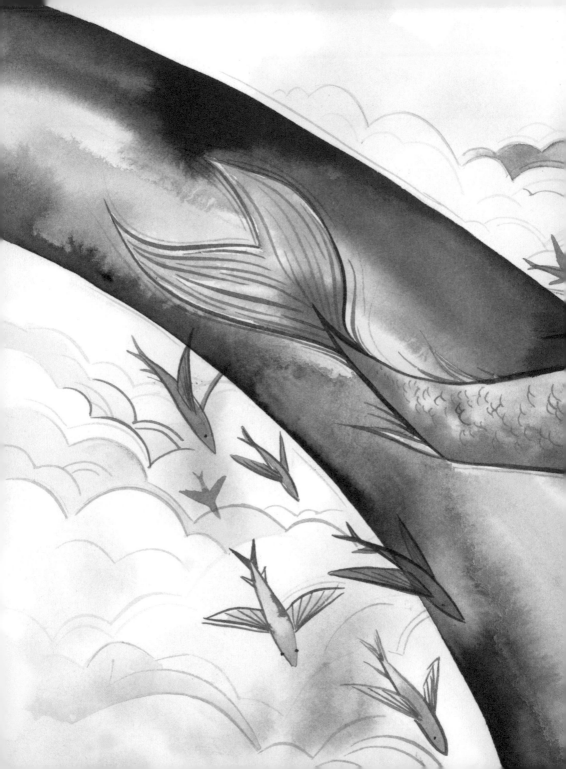

It travels by

RAINBOW

and summons groups of flying fish…

KILLING

anyone who crosses its path.

ENENRA

Light a

BONFIRE

in Japan and you may summon this

SMOKE
MONSTER...

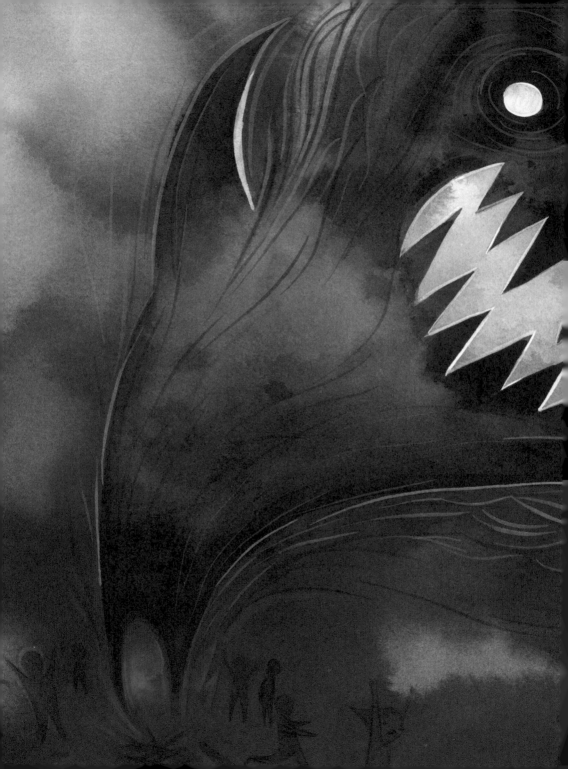

It is

HARMLESS

and just wants to be your friend.

SHADHAVAR

You may

HEAR

this Persian unicorn before you

SEE IT...

Its

HOLLOW HORN

plays music when the wind blows,
drawing in creatures from miles around.

It is also

CARNIVOROUS.

NINKI NANKA

This

WATER DRAGON

lives in the

SWAMPS

of West Africa...

Where it
PUNISHES
disobedient children.

ALP

This monstrous creature

SNEAKS INTO HOMES

in Germany...

SHAPESHIFT

or even turn
INVISIBLE.

It drinks human blood and causes terrible
NIGHTMARES...

But is

HELPLESS

without its magic hat.

ACKNOWLEDGMENTS

Many thanks go out to the Chronicle team, especially my wonderful editor Julia Patrick. To my parents who always inspired interest and wonder in the strange and bizarre, to Cliff Mitchell who has been a huge support through this creative endeavor, and to the little beastling whose due date has kept me on track of my deadlines.

THE AUTHOR

Emma SanCartier is a monster-obsessed illustrator and sculptor whose work has been featured in children's books, magazines, and gallery shows. Originally from northern Ontario, she currently lives in Seattle.